Bonnie's Rocket

by Emeline Lee   *illustrated by* Alina Chau

Lee & Low Books Inc.
New York

Bonnie was designing a magnificent rocket ship…

FIN

ROCKET
BODY

NOSE CONE

Baba was an engineer for NASA's Apollo 11 space mission.

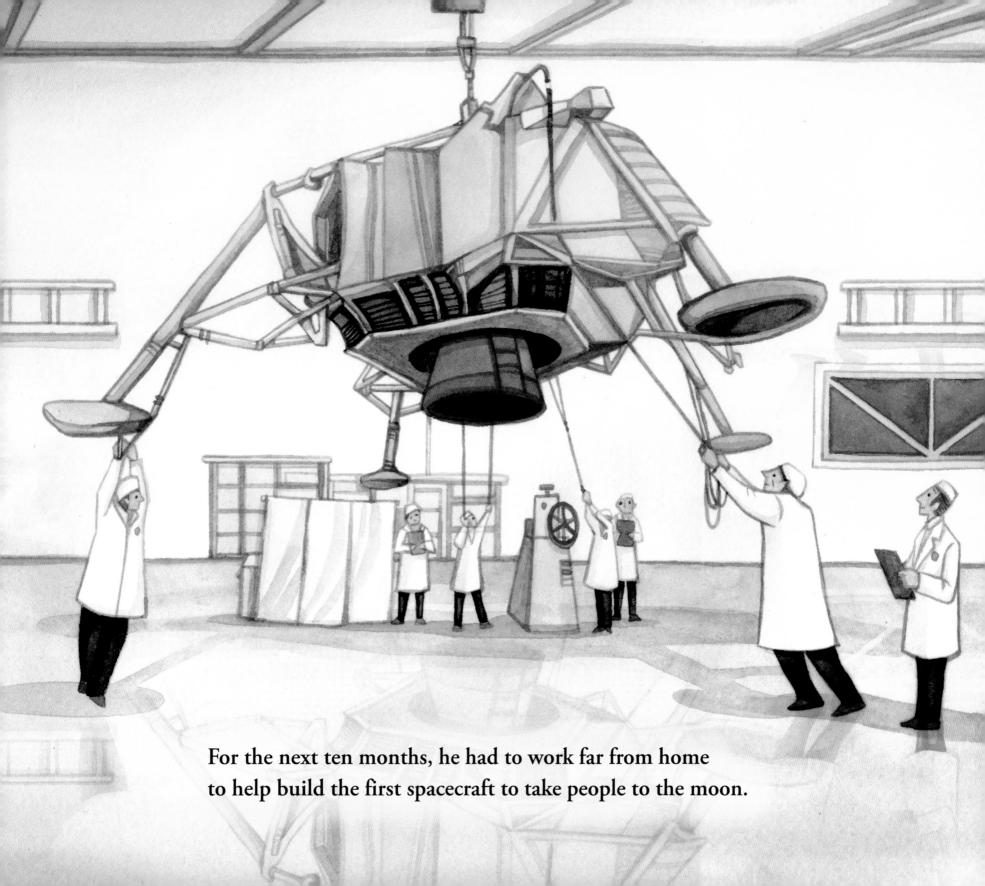

For the next ten months, he had to work far from home
to help build the first spacecraft to take people to the moon.

① DESIGN

② BUILD

90°

Tin can

SOUP

Materials

* tin can
* cardboard
* duct tape
* paper clips
* sticks
* rubber bands

Before he left, Baba gave Bonnie an engineering notebook to record her progress toward a successful rocket launch. She planned to show him the spectacular results when he returned. It would take a lot of work, but Bonnie loved a challenge.

Still, Bonnie missed Baba. She missed laughing at his funny stories. She missed bike riding to the park together. But most of all, she missed talking with him about everything from fluffy pancakes to far-off planets.

One day, she received a letter in the mail.

October 25, 1968

Dear Bonnie,

I've missed you, Mei Mei, and Mama very much since I've been away. At the Space Center, we've just completed the Apollo 7 mission, which sent three astronauts into orbit around Earth. The astronauts spent eleven days in space to test the ship before we try for the moon. How's your rocket coming along?

Love,

Baba

Bonnie soon finished Stage 1 of her project, the Design.
She jumped straight into Stage 2, the Build.

December 18, 1968

Dear Bonnie,

I wish I could be home with you for Christmas, but we're on a tight schedule to finish the spacecraft in time for the launch. The astronauts are depending on us to build a safe ship, so we are testing every part thoroughly. Although we're not together this year, I'm sending you a special present and a big warm hug.

Love,

Baba

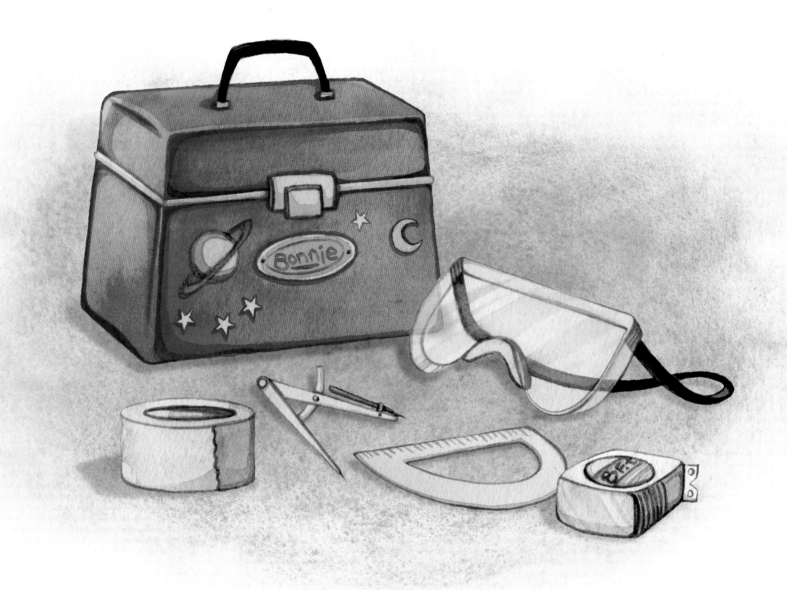

When Bonnie opened Baba's gift, she discovered an engineer's treasure chest: a compass and protractor, along with a tape measure, safety goggles, and a huge roll of duct tape. It was exactly what she needed to complete her ship!

Just like Baba worked with a team of engineers . . .

...Bonnie had a team of her own. Once she and her friends finished building the ship, they prepared for Stage 3, the Test.

They set up the slingshot and counted down the launch....

But the rocket did not travel very far at all.

February 7, 1969

Dear Bonnie,

I'm sorry to hear that your first rocket launch wasn't successful. But even NASA's best engineers have to test their rockets many times over before they work properly. Each test reveals clues about what needs fixing. Keep up the good work!

Love,

Baba

When Bonnie and her friends completed Stage 4, the Analysis, they realized their rocket needed a stronger boost. Bonnie remembered a model volcano that she made once with Baba. Using baking soda and vinegar, she could create a fizzy chemical reaction that would shoot the rocket up into the sky.

But the blast turned out to be a little *too* explosive.
Now they had to start all over again.

April 15, 1969

Dear Bonnie,

Don't be discouraged by going back to the beginning. Remember that the engineering process can take a while for anyone—NASA's teams have been working on Project Apollo for years! It may take some time and patience, but I know you'll figure it out.

Love,

Baba

The next day, as Bonnie biked home from school, she hit a bump in the road. Air hissed out of the tire. Everything seemed to be going wrong.

After patching up her tire, Bonnie used a pump to inflate it.
The rush of air gave her a new idea for the rocket launch.

Bonnie and her friends crafted a brand-new rocket ship.

They poured some water inside it and used the bike pump to fill it with air. The pressure within the ship built and built until...

...the rocket sprang up on a jet of mist. Eureka!

June 26, 1969

Dear Bonnie,

Congratulations! I can't wait to see your rocket reach the sky! And your ideas for cutting down the weight to achieve even more height next time sound very promising. At Mission Control, we are at T-minus 20 days until the Apollo 11 launch. We're all a bit nervous about the moon landing, but I have a good feeling about it.

Love,

Baba

Finally, the day of the Apollo 11 launch arrived. Everyone watched as the enormous rocket lifted off in a billowing cloud of smoke.

After the astronauts returned safely to Earth,
Baba came home at last.

Everyone gathered in the backyard
for the long-awaited launch of Bonnie's rocket.

"Bonnie, you've built an extraordinary rocket ship!" Baba said. "And you still have some blank pages left in your engineering notebook."

"I already have an idea for my next project," she told him.

It would take a lot of work, but Bonnie loved a challenge.

How to Build a Rocket Like Bonnie's Sky Voyager

Note: This project requires adult supervision when using sharp objects and conducting the launch.
Make sure to launch the rocket ship in an open area without obstructions overhead.

Materials:

Scissors
Cardboard
Duct tape
1-liter plastic bottle
Box cutter
Cork
Awl
Water
Bicycle tire pump with inflating needle

For more on how to make your own bottle rocket and the scientific principles behind Bonnie's different launching techniques, visit EmelineLee.com.

Instructions

1. Cut four identical fins from the cardboard and tape them to the bottle so they extend about four inches above the opening.

2. Use the box cutter to halve the cork. With the awl, poke a small hole down the center of one half.

3. Fill one-third of the bottle with water and plug the mouth with the cork with the hole in it.

4. Thread the needle of the tire pump through the cork's hole before turning the bottle upside down and resting the fins on level ground.

5. Give the pump a series of quick, strong pushes to fill the rocket with air.

6. Watch your rocket ship launch into the sky!

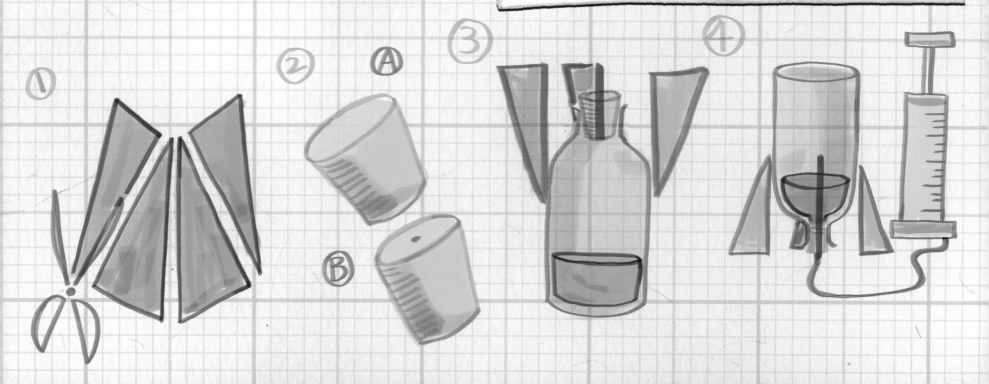

Author's Note

The story of Bonnie and Baba is inspired by the life of my grandfather, Lau Tung Kwan, who worked as an engineer for the Apollo 11 space mission, during which astronauts first landed on the moon. He was born in Guangzhou, China, in 1929 and immigrated to the United States at age twenty-three to pursue job opportunities and support his family. In the mid-1960s, he began working at the Grumman Aerospace Corporation in Bethpage, New York, where he and his team helped design and build Lunar Modules (LM) for NASA's Apollo space program. The first LM to transport astronauts to the surface of the moon was named the *Eagle*.

My grandfather's team of engineers was responsible for designing the life-support systems in the LM and the space suits worn by the astronauts. Even in the excitement of implementing new technologies for the space program, he was always guided by the motto "Human safety comes first." His job required him to spend some time away from his family, traveling between the Kennedy Space Center in Merritt Island, Florida, and the Mission Control Center in Houston, Texas. From the launch on July 16, 1969 until splashdown eight days later, he remained on call with Mission Control to help monitor the temperature, air pressure, humidity, and oxygen supply levels within the space suits and the LM.

In addition to the success of the first lunar landing, my grandfather's other memorable experiences include the Apollo 13 mission, during which an oxygen tank unexpectedly exploded on the main spacecraft while in space. The accident forced the astronauts to rely on the LM as their lifeline, and my grandfather was one of the engineers who helped Mission Control manage the LM's oxygen supply during the perilous journey home. The safe return of the Apollo 13 crew amid dire circumstances remains one of NASA's greatest achievements.

The Apollo space program demonstrated the power of a diverse nation working together toward a common goal. The program's legacy continues to fuel dreams of space exploration and inspire current and future generations of innovators to push the boundaries of scientific discovery and cooperation.

*To Ye Ye and Ma Ma, who always inspire me
to shoot for the moon.*

—*E. L.*

To my mom and dad, who encourage me to dream big!

—*A. C.*

LEE & LOW BOOKS Inc., 95 Madison Avenue, New York, NY 10016
leeandlow.com
Edited by Cheryl Klein
Book design by Sheila Smallwood
Book production by The Kids at Our House
The text is set in Adobe Garamond Pro Semibold with display type in Coconut Punch.
The illustrations were completed in watercolor on paper and Photoshop.
Manufactured in China by RR Donnelley
10 9 8 7 6 5 4 3 2 1
First Edition

FSC® MIX
Paper from responsible sources
www.fsc.org FSC® C144853

Cataloging-in-Publication data is on file with the Library of Congress.
ISBN 978-1-64379-069-5